DATE DUE		

Kim Jernigan of *The New Quarterly* describes John Metcalf as 'a self-confessed lover of words, a delightful and delighted prose stylist, a missionary anthologist, a mischievous and unsparing critic of Canadian literature and literary culture, and a writer of fiction that can slide indiscernibly from comic petulance to pointed satire to something more passionate and poignant.'

'One of Canada's best kept literary secrets ...'
   – *Harper's Bazaar*

'... hilarious, touching and delightful ... brilliant concision and understated humor.' – *Los Angeles Times*

'His talent is generous, hectoring, huge and remarkable.'
   – *The Washington Post*

'As a comic writer, as a satirist and as a sensitive recorder of human passion, Metcalf is highly skilled.... [His fiction] is a tonic antidote ... to the earnestness and torpor of so much of our good-for-you canon.' – Russell Smith

Forde Abroad

Forde Abroad

John Metcalf

a novella

The Porcupine's Quill

NATIONAL LIBRARY OF CANADA
CATALOGUING IN PUBLICATION DATA

Metcalf, John, 1938–
    Forde abroad/John Metcalf.

ISBN 0-88984-266-3

I. Title.

PS8576.E83F67 2003   C813'.54   C2003-900942-4
PR9199.3.M45F67 2003

Published by The Porcupine's Quill, www.sentex.net/~pql
68 Main Street, Erin, Ontario NOB ITO.

Represented in Canada by the Literary Press Group.
Trade orders are available from University of Toronto Press.

We acknowledge the support of the Ontario Arts Council, and
the Canada Council for the Arts for our publishing program.
The financial support of the Government of Canada through
the Book Publishing Industry Development Program
is also gratefully acknowledged. Thanks, also,
to the Government of Ontario through the
Ontario Media Development Corporation's
Ontario Book Initiative.

Canadä

For Myrna

ROAST PORK WITH CRACKLING WAS REPELLENT. Roast pork with crackling was *goyishe dreck.* Black Forest ham with Swiss cheese was, however, her favourite kind of sandwich. She loved even the greasiest of salamis. Sausages, on the other hand, were unclean. All Chinese food involving pork was perfectly acceptable with the single exception of steamed minced pork which was, apparently, vile *trayf* of the most abhorrent kind. Prosciutto she adored. But pork chops … *feh!*

Forde stared at Sheila in exasperation.

'And you can be sure they haven't changed,' she said, 'in their hearts.'

'But how do you know they ever *were* …'

'But how do you know they weren't?'

'Well, I don't, but how *could* they have deported anyone? Slovenia was invaded by the Nazis. The Slovenians were a subject people. Slovenia was an occupied country just as – as France was.'

'And look at *their* record.'

'I don't think,' he said, 'that this is a particularly logical conversation.'

Lines at the corners of her eyes tightened.

'So what makes you think they didn't collaborate? Like the whatnames.'

'Which whatnames?'

'The French ones. Begins with M.'

'The *milice?*'

'Exactly.'

'Well, I *don't* know …'

'More likely than not, I'd say.'

'… but I'll look it up,' he said.

She bent over the atlas again.

'Here's the Nazis immediately north of them in Austria.

And then immediately to the right of them in Hungary – what were those called? The Iron Cross? The Iron Guard?'

'I think it was the Arrowcross.'

With her left shoulder she gave a quick, irritated shrug.

'And then *here* to the south of them you've got the Ustashi in Croatia. Why *should* the Slovenians have been any different?'

'Listen,' he said, 'Sheila …'

'But, please,' she said, 'it's your career. I know I'm just being silly.'

She patted below her eyes with a tissue.

'If it's what you want, off you go.'

She sniffed.

'Off you go,' she said, her voice breaking.

'Sheila … *please*.'

'No!' she said fiercely. 'No! You can go there and you can do what you want. I don't care. I don't *care* if you choose to consort with Slovenians.'

To her offended and retreating back, he said, 'I hardly think the word "consort" is quite … oh, *indescribable* BALLS!'

AFTER SHE HAD LEFT FOR WORK, Forde stood over the toilet in the second floor bathroom. The intense, rich yellow, the Day-Glo brightness of his urine, gave him daily pleasure. The vitamins did it. He wasn't sure if it was the E, the beta carotene, the C or the Megavits. He had read in a newspaper article that vitamins C and E 'captured free radicals'; he had no idea what that meant and wasn't curious but he enjoyed the sound of it. It made him think of warfare against insurgent forces in fetid jungles, sibilant native blades, *parang* and *kris*.

Even the toilet itself pleased him. It was probably seventy or eighty years old. Against the back of the bowl in purple script was the word 'Vitreous.' And above that in a wreath of what might have been acanthus leaves was the toilet's name – 'Prompto'.

He flushed the toilet and watched his brightness diluted, swirled away. He stood looking at himself in the medicine cabinet mirror as the plumbing groaned and water rilled and spirted, silence rising, settling.

He wandered into his frowsty study and sat at his ugly government-surplus oak desk. Beyond its far edge the scabby radiator. Then the blank wall. Two years earlier he had faced the window but had spent too much time gazing out watching passersby and the busyness of dogs.

Usually he enjoyed the daily solitude and drew the deepening silence of the house around him like a blanket. But on this day the silence burdened him. He sat looking down at the gold-plated stem-winder which always lay flat on the desk to his right. He wound it every morning, pleased every morning by the feel of the knurled winding-knob. He had bought it at a pawn shop cheaply because engraved on the back of the watch were the words: *Presented to George Pepper in recognition of forty-five years service to the Canadian Cardboard Box Company.*

It amused him to think that this was the only presentation

gold watch he'd ever have. No such flourishes were likely to conclude *his* career. He kept the watch on the desk as a talisman, a spur to effort, as *memento mori*, as a reminder of the world to which he gratefully did not belong. He thought of the watch as 'George'. He sometimes talked to it.

This is a lovely bit of writing, George, even if I say so myself. And why not? No one else will.

I think we can get another hour in, George, before we're completely knackered.

He wound the watch.

He sighed.

He sat staring across his desk's familiar clutter. He had no appetite for writing necessary letters, for providing references and recommendations, for the fiddle of filing. His last novel was now six months behind him – almost a year since he'd written seriously – but he remained listless, uncommitted about what he might do next, bored.

When he was in the grip of first-draft writing, he risked nothing that might break the flow. Ritual and omen ruled. He laid in stocks of Branston pickle, wooden matches, tins of Medaglia d'Oro. His heart leapt at the cawing of crows. He did not like to leave the house, did not open his mail, did not shower, wash or shave, slept in unchanged shirt and underpants, sat in his study smelling the smell of himself.

It was only on Friday mornings that this obsessive routine was interrupted. On Friday mornings the cleaning lady hired by Sheila arrived at nine and made his life unendurable until noon. He had begged and remonstrated, but Sheila had offered as the only alternative that he clean the house himself as she had neither the time nor the energy. And definitely no inclination. He saw fully the justice of her position but felt put upon.

He attempted politeness when he let the woman in, attempted conversations about the weather, the heat, the cold, the damp, but could never understand more than a word in five of anything she said. Although he closed his study door and put on his industrial ear-mufflers, he could still hear her imprecations and mad Portuguese diatribes, her crooning monologues punctuated by sudden squawks and screeches directed at vacuum cleaner or door knob.

She had once left a note on the kitchen counter which read: *Mis mis erclen finisples.*

It had worried at him most of the afternoon.

Sheila had read it with impatient ease. *Miss. Mister Clean is finished, please.*

According to Sheila, Mrs Silva had an unemployed husband with three toes missing on one foot from an industrial accident, a son who was a bad lot, and was herself a devoutly Catholic hypochondriac whose spare time was divided equally between her priest and doctor.

He could not understand how Sheila had found any of this out, how she understood anything the bloody woman said, but he had come to suspect that Sheila's ability to understand Mrs Silva, bereaved Romanian upholsterers, and monoglot Vietnamese shelf-stockers in odoriferous Asian stores had less to do with some rare linguistic talent than it had to do with the fact that she was a nicer person than he was.

He started to link up the doodles.

One of John D. MacDonald's thrillers came into his mind. He'd always admired the title: *The Girl, the Gold Watch, and Everything.*

He was supposed to be polishing an interview which was supposed to appear in the summer issue of *Harvest,* but *Harvest* was doubtless two issues behind where it was supposed to be so that all of its three hundred subscribers would have to wait with bated breath until the summer of *next* year before they could devour his profound and penetrating insights into this, that and whatever, so that, all in all, six of this and half a dozen of the other, all things being equal, when push came to shove, polishing the bloody thing up did not seem an enterprise.

'... of great pith and moment,' he declaimed into the study's silence.

Who *said* that?

Fortinbras?

Hamlet himself?

He plodded downstairs to find a copy of *The Complete Plays* and to make a cup of tea. Better for his health, Sheila insisted, than coffee.

I must put my pyjamas, he chanted, *in the drawer marked pyjamas.*

I must eat my charcoal biscuit, he recited, *which is good for me.*

As he stood waiting for the kettle to boil, he looked at the *New York Times Atlas of the World* Sheila had left open on the counter. He took a roll of Magic Tape from the kitchen drawer and started to tape up the tears in the tattered blue dust jacket; he'd been meaning to do that for weeks. Often after dinner they sat over the atlas finishing the wine and squabbling happily over holidays they would never be able to afford. Sheila's most recent creation had been a trip up the Nile to see the temples but without getting off the boat because Egypt was hot and smelly and every historical site was plagued by importunate dragomen, smelly and anti-semites to a man, and one could surely get a *sense* of the temples while remaining in one's deck chair and being served large Bombay gin martinis.

A snort of laughter escaped him as he thought of the words 'consort with Slovenians'.

Her performance that morning had not, of course, been about Slovenians, World War II fascist groups or deported Jews. It had been what he thought shrinks called 'displacement'. It was that, simply, she was upset that he was going away and although she had not yet said so, she was even more upset that at the conference he would for the first time be meeting Karla.

14

Sheila did not like Karla. She had taken against her from the arrival of the first letter. She always referred to her as 'your Commie pen pal'.

The conference was to be held in the Alps at a lake resort called Splad. The brochure about the hotel and its services was written in an English which charmed him. He thought it strange that in a Communist country a hotel would offer to launder silk handkerchiefs; they also offered to launder Gentlemen Linen and Nightshirsts. He had studied the sample menus with fascination; he particularly liked the sound of National Beans with Pork Jambs. It seemed certain that the whole expedition would provide him with unimaginable comic material.

But he had scarcely bothered to glance at the programme itself when it had arrived from the Literary and Cultural Association of Slovenia, disliking the hairy East European paper it was printed on and the fact that the paper was not the normal 8 1/2 by 11 inches but 8 1/2 by 11 3/4, an intensely irritating deviation probably traceable, like the metric system, to the meddling of Napoleon.

From horrid experience, he knew that the papers would range from deconstructionist babble to weird explications in uncertain English of the profundities of Mazo de la Roche and Lucy Maud Montgomery.

Not that he would be caught listening to any of it; he would rather, he thought, sit and listen to a washing machine.

And ranged between the deconstructionists and the simply uncomprehending there would be interminable feminists in frocks and army boots, gay theorists in bright green leather shoes, huddles of Slovenians in suits discussing Truth, the State, the Writer, smart-alec Marxist smarty-boots, chaps in tweed from New Zealand....

But looking on the bright side, his expenses in Slovenia would be covered by the Literary and Cultural Association, and his travel expenses to Slovenia would be covered by the

Department of External Affairs which was also to pay him a *per diem* and a small honorarium. This, together with another honorarium from the Slovenians for reading, might mean returning home five hundred dollars ahead.

And he'd be freed from his desk, from the chipped radiator, the blank wall facing; he'd be free of the house, he'd be out and about, out in the world, free of the weight of his numbing routines.

His spirits rose at the thought of leaving behind the wearying end of Ottawa's winter, the snow beginning now its slow retreat revealing Listerine bottles and dog turds. He would be leaving behind brown bare twigs and flying towards a world in leaf, in the alpine meadows, gentians.

And once ensconced in Splad, he would perhaps meet someone who would wish to write about his work. Perhaps a convivial evening in the bar might lead to further translation.... Nor could he deny that he enjoyed the attention, couldn't deny that it made him feel expansive to answer questions, pontificate, disparage Robertson Davies.

'What I don't understand,' Sheila had said, probing at his contradictions to deflate and anger him in these last bickering days before his flight, 'what I can't follow is why it gives you pleasure to impress people for whom you have little or no respect. Why *is* that?'

'Well, it's not so much the *people*,' he'd explained, 'it's what they represent.'

'And what's that?'

'Well ... a certain interest, a respect even ... these are academics from all over the world, you know.'

'And according to you some of them can't speak English and the rest talk gibberish.'

'I'm not saying it's a *desirable* situation, Sheila, but one's reputation rests to a certain extent on how much attention academics pay to one's work.'

'One's reputation does, does it?'

He had shaken his head slowly to convey a weary dignity.

'And one doesn't feel,' she'd probed further, 'that disporting oneself in front of people one disdains is rather … well … *pitiable?*'

He sighed and sipped at the tea.

Lighted a luxurious cigarette.

Closed the atlas.

And there also awaited in Splad the pleasure of holding in his hands a translation into Serbian of his third novel, *Winter Creatures*. His translator was travelling to Splad from Belgrade bringing the book with him. At a conference two years earlier in Italy he'd been approached by a man – and actually he wouldn't swear to the *absolute* details of any of this because he'd been rather drunk himself and had not quite grasped everything the man was saying, what with the noise in the bar and the accent and the syntax – by a man whose father was Serbian and whose mother was Croatian – or possibly it was the other way round – who worked for a cultural radio station and magazine in Belgrade and who was an actor and impresario who translated works in English into Serbian on behalf of the Writers of Serbia Cultural Association and who, when not involved in manifestations, worked by day as chauffeur to a man of extensive power.

After his return to Canada, Forde had largely forgotten this loud stranger with his winks and nods, his glittering gold fillings, his finger tapping the side of his nose, until the telephone calls began.

Ripped from sleep at 3:33, heart pounding, staring into the digital clock inches from his face, Forde croaked into the phone.

'Hello?' he repeated.

'Here is Drago.'

'Who?'

'*Drago! Drago!*'

'*Who is it?*'

He flapped his hand at her.

3:34

'You will visit me in Beograd. We will have much talking.'

'Beograd?'

'*Yes!* Yes, Robert Forde.'

'Excuse me ... you're ... from Bologna?'

'Yes, *certainly* Bologna.'

'I'm sorry. For a moment, I ... ah ... rather disoriented.'

3:35

'In Beograd we will together drink Nescafé.'

This had been the first of many calls.

All came in the small hours.

'Get *his* fucking number!' hissed Sheila, furiously humping the sheets over her shoulder. 'I'll phone *him* in the middle of *his* fucking night, fucking Slav fuckheads.'

Forde soon came to dread that ruthless, domineering voice. Drago bombarded, hectored, rode roughshod.

He was implacable.

He was impervious.

'Here is Drago. You have written: "American students littered the steps." This *littered* is not a nice word, not a *possible* word, it is meaning *excrement* and *rubbish* and so would *offend* the Americans so we find a *compromise* word....'

He wondered what the book would look like. He presumed it would be a paperback but didn't know whether they went in for the quality paperback format or whether they produced paperbacks in the utilitarian French style. He realized that he didn't even know if Serbian was written in the Roman alphabet or in Cyrillic. He wondered what Serbian readers would make of *Winter Creatures* given Drago's strange queries and frequent assurances that he would 'make things come nice'. He suspected that the novel had been less translated than traduced. So why was he so gratified to have his novel badly translated into a language he couldn't read?

Forde did not delude himself.

He had not forgotten the wellingtons phone call.

'Wellies,' said Drago. 'This means, I think, *venery.*'

'*What?*'

'You *know*, Robert Forde, what I am saying.'

'No, *no*, Drago! Wellies are rubber boots.'

He had listened to the echoic international silence.

'Short for wellingtons.'

'Never,' said Drago, 'in all my reading and my talking, *never* have I heard it called so.'

'*It?*' he'd squeaked.

But he *was* gratified. As he sat doodling at his desk, he hummed. Had he liked cigars, he would have smoked one. Had there been a mirror in his study, he would have inclined his head with all the benign courtesy of a grandee.

'… consort with Slovenians.…'

He grinned at the radiator.

He was even pleased by Sheila's moody assaults, pleased and a little flattered that after all the years they'd been together she could still flame into jealousy. Not that she had the slightest cause for concern. As he'd told her repeatedly, his friendship with Karla was a purely literary friendship.

Her first letter had arrived some three years ago from the University of Jena in the German Democratic Republic. She had expressed her admiration of his novels – a colleague at the University of Augsburg had lent her some volumes – and although her syntax and vocabulary were sometimes peculiar, he'd been pleased to receive her praise. No one from East Germany had ever written to him before. She had ended her letter by saying that her great sorrow was that she had not been able to read his first two novels because she could not obtain them. Was it possible he could send her copies? For such a resolution of the problem she would be most grateful.

'Why has it always got to be *you*?' Sheila demanded. 'Why should *you* have to pay for the books and postage?'

'Well, I've never thought about it before but I don't think their currency trades. They can't buy things with it in the west.'

'Well, how did her letter get here then, with an East German stamp on it?'

'I don't know. I don't know how that works.'

'Well,' said Sheila. 'I'd say there something suspicious about it.'

He had sent her the books and within weeks they were writing back and forth regularly. What other Canadian writers should she read? Who were reliable critics? Which books were most loved by the Canadian people? She loved to read about Red Indians and Eskimos and the North. Was Grey Owl thought a great Canadian writer? Canadians, as she had studied in Margaret Atwood's book *Survival*, had invented the genre of the wild animal story. Should she read Ernest Thompson Seton? An anthology at the University contained an Ernest Thompson Seton story entitled 'Raggylug, the Story of a Cottontail Rabbit'. Was this one of his most loved stories?

Forde had dealt with all this misplaced enthusiasm firmly. He had explained that no books were beloved of the Canadian people with the sole exception of *Anne of Green Gables* and that only because it had been on television. Most Canadians, he had explained, were functionally illiterate. No stories by Ernest Thompson Seton were 'most loved' because only academics knew who he was.

He explained that most Eskimos worked in collectives with power tools turning out soapstone seals. The North was actually a vast slum run by the federal government's Canadian Mortgage and Housing Corporation, the landscape littered with empty oil barrels. There *were* Red Indians but no longer of the bow-and-arrow variety. They were not to be called 'Red' Indians. Indeed, they were not to be called 'Indians'. In Ottawa, people of the First Nations wearing traditional braids and cowboy boots were almost bound to be high-priced, hotshot lawyers.

He began to send her reading lists; in the library he xeroxed what critical articles he could stomach; he sent clippings and reviews. When he went out walking around Ottawa's used-book stores, he picked up inexpensive paperbacks and from time to time sent parcels.

After a few months had gone by, he felt bold enough to start correcting her English.

The more he moulded and shaped her, the larger the claims her letters made on him. She became increasingly confident of his attention. Her ardent engagement with his own writing slightly embarrassed him. It seemed a natural progression for his letters to move from *Sincerely* to *With best wishes* to *With warm regards* to *Affectionately*. He had hesitated before writing *With love* and had then delayed mailing the letter.

During the two weeks he waited for her reply he found that the letter and her possible reactions to it came often into his mind.

He asked no questions about her life but often as he sat staring across the grain of the government-surplus desk made uglier by thick polyurethane, he found himself wandering, daydreaming.

He had gleaned some few facts about her. He imagined that she must be between thirty-five and forty because she had a son aged ten. She had not mentioned a husband; when she used the word 'we' she always seemed to mean herself and the boy. She lived in an apartment in an old house. She used the spare bedroom as her study.

When Sheila commented on the flow of letters from the German Democratic Republic, he had explained to her that such contacts were simply a normal part of the literary life, a necessary part of the shape of a career.

After they had been corresponding for about a year, there

arrived in the week before Christmas a padded airmail package fastened in European style with split brass pins. It contained between two sheets of cardboard a photograph of Karla and a Christmas card drawn by Viktor of the Three Magi and what was probably a camel.

The photograph was a glossy close-up studio portrait in black and white and lighted in a stilted and old-fashioned style. Karla was in dramatic profile gazing up towards the upper left-hand corner. It reminded Forde of a Hollywood publicity photo from the forties of some such star as Joan Crawford or Myrna Loy.

Embarrassed that Sheila should see it, he said, 'What a strange thing to send someone!'

'Fancies herself, doesn't she?' said Sheila.

'But going to a *studio*,' said Forde.

Sheila tilted the photo.

'Probably air-brushed,' she said, dropping it on the counter.

Pointing at the camel, he said, 'What do you think that is?'

'I just wonder,' she said, 'what you'll get next.'

What he got next was a request for three tubes of Revlon Color Stay lipstick: No. 41 'Blush', No. 04 'Nude', and No. 42 'Flesh'. He had lurked along the cosmetics counters in Eaton's in the Rideau Centre trying to avoid the eye of any of their attendant beauticians. He knew these supercilious women with their improbable sculpted make-up thought him a pervert, the Eaton's equivalent of the schoolyard's man-in-a-mac. He had felt uncomfortable and faintly guilty while buying the lipsticks but later felt even guiltier about not telling Sheila.

But he had done no wrong. He had to insist on that. It was not being disloyal to describe Sheila as in certain ways excitable. There was simply no point in upsetting her needlessly. Where lay the fault in buying small gifts for a friend – a colleague – who lived under a repressive totalitarian regime which did not allow her access to such simple commodities as lipstick? Or the Ysatis perfume by Givenchy she'd later requested?

He opened his desk drawer and took out the calendar. He had put the photograph inside the calendar to keep it flat. He looked at the upturned face. He looked at the dark fall of hair. Her lips were slightly parted. Light glistened on the fullness of her bottom lip. It was as if seconds before the photographer had pressed the shutter-release button, she had run her tongue across her lip wetting it.

He put the photograph back in the calendar.

Tearing off the doodles page from his writing pad and the page beneath where the ink had gone through, he started to jot down all the words in German he could think of. He couldn't think of many. He arranged them into alphabetical order and sat looking at the result.

Autobahn	*Kristallnacht*
Blitz	*Luftwaffe*
dankeschön	*Panzer*
ersatz	*Realpolitik*
Flak	*Reich*
Führer	*Stalag*
Gauleiter	*Übermensch*
Gestapo	*Waffen SS*
Kaiser	*auf Wiedersehen*

SHEILA WAS PRETENDING to be concentrating on driving. From Ottawa International Airport he was to fly to Toronto on the Air Canada Rapidair service. In Toronto he was to board a Lufthansa flight to Frankfurt. In Frankfurt he was to board a JAT flight for Slovenia's capital, Ljubljana. He stared out of the window at the wastes of snow, the frozen trees, the roadside lines of piled crud left by the snowplough. From time to time Sheila sniffed.

'All this stuff's of your own imagining, you know.'

She did not reply.

'Sheila?'

'I've said what I had to say, thank you.'

'Yes, but it was untrue and unfair.'

As the road curved round to the parking and departures area, Sheila said, 'I'll drop you off at the Air Canada counters and then I won't have to bother with parking.'

'And also,' he said, 'hurtful.'

She pulled the car in to the curb and parked.

'Well ...,' said Forde.

'Have a good trip,' she said.

'Aren't you going to kiss me goodbye?'

She inclined her head towards him and he found his lips brushing her cheek.

He gathered his carry-on bag, umbrella, and briefcase and opening the car door said, 'Really, Sheila, you're being ridiculous.'

She sat staring ahead.

He got out and shut the door.

Stood for a moment.

Started across the sidewalk to the revolving door.

Sheila leaned across the passenger seat and wound down the window. She called out to him.

'Pardon?'

'*Az der putz shtait ...*'

'What?'

'*Az der putz shtait ligt doss saichel in tuchus.*'

'What's that mean?'

She turned the key in the ignition.

'*What did that mean?*'

He reached for the door handle.

She pushed down the button locking all the doors.

He banged on the roof of the car with the flat of his hand. She rolled up the window.

'*I demand to know what that meant!*'

A small male child with a suitcase on wheels stopped to gape up at him.

A Blue Line cab driver parked behind them had lowered his window and was staring.

'*What did that mean?*'

He emphasized each word by accompanying it with a bash on the car's hood with the malacca handle of his umbrella.

The taxi driver started honking his horn.

Sheila stretched across the passenger seat and opened the window two or three inches. Hoisting the strap of the carry-on bag higher on his shoulder and jamming the briefcase under his arm, Forde stooped to confront her through the narrow slot.

'It's an old Yiddish saying.'

Forde glared.

'*Az der putz shtait* … When the prick stands up,' she said, '… *ligt doss saichel in tuchus* … the brains sink into the ass.'

THE ORNATE IRON LAMP POSTS along the lake's margin speared light out on the water. Gravel crunched under their feet. Somewhere out beyond the reach of the lamps a waterfowl beat a brief commotion in the water. After the heat and the blare and the smoke of the crowded bars in the dining room, the breeze from the lake smelled invigoratingly boggy.

'Intrigue,' continued Christopher, 'will be rampant.'

He wiggled his fingers like fishes.

'Aswirl with currents.'

'But who's listening? Does anyone really *care* what academics say?'

'*Everybody* is listening, Robert. This isn't Canada. Much of what's going on here you won't be able to understand. But the Party is listening, the factions of the separatists are listening, the Croatians are listening, the Serbs, the Macedonians, a positive *stew* of intelligence people.... And there are Slovenian writers here, too. They're important political figures, spokespeople. You see, writing here *is* politics.'

With Christopher Harris, Forde felt he had hit the mother lode. They had sat together on the bus which had carried the party from the Ljubljana Holiday Inn to Splad and had quickly fallen into delighted conversation. Christopher was, Forde assumed, gay, about Forde's age, his nose blooming with drink-burst veins, and his fingernails all bitten to the quick. He was a British expatriate who lived and taught in Lund in Sweden – *Provincial. Something of a backwater of a university, really. I'm suited* – but who was an expert on all things Yugoslavian. His passion in life was the celebration of Slovenia and the Slovene language; he had translated most of the significant literature; he was working on a history.

Slovenians, Christopher had explained, considered themselves strongly European, a civilized, energetic northern people distinct from the increasingly dubious rabble to be found to the south, a rabble which culminated in the barbarism and squalor of Islam. This did not mean, Christopher had insisted, that the Slovenians were any more racist than anyone else. Exactly the same sentiments were openly expressed in Germany, France and Italy. Try cashing a cheque issued in Rome in a bank in Milan without having to listen to an earful about the duplicity of idle southern monkeys.

Christopher had also explained that although the ostensible purpose of the conference was to discuss matters Canadian, much of the international presence was also intended by the organizers as a buffer and defence for separatist Slovenians who would slant their papers and statements in politically unacceptable directions.

Secession was in the air.

They turned back towards the hotel, Christopher sparkling off fact and anecdote – Saint Cyril, called in earlier life Constantine, the Glagolitic alphabet, the battles of Kosovo and Lepanto, the quirks of Selim the Terrible, the westernmost reaches of the Ottoman Empire, the karst cave system near Ljubljana, Chetniks, fourteenth-century church frescos – pausing only to sing sad stanzas from a Slovenian folk song about boys leaving their sweethearts to suffer their forced military service in the Austro-Hungarian army.

''Alf a mo', squire,' he said in a sudden Cockney whine.

He stood with his back to Forde and pissed loudly on a bush.

Forde suddenly felt shivery cold and quite drunk.

The verb 'to stale' came into his mind.

He had had some powerful short brown drinks commended by Christopher and two bottles of nasty wine.

Christopher's feet on the gravel again.

'That mansion set back there,' he said, pointing, 'was one of ex-King Peter's summer palaces. Do you know Cecil Parrott?
Chap who translated *The Good Soldier Švejk* for Penguin? When he was a young man, he was tutor in that house to the two Crown Princes. Tiny, the literary world, isn't it?'

The bulk of the hotel was looming in the darkness. It was a strange building, its central block the remains of a massively built castle which according to Christopher dated from the fifteenth century. In the nineteen-thirties, an architect had joined onto the existing structure three huge concrete and glass wings. They rose up into the air like birds' wings, rather like, Forde thought, three immense upside-down Stealth aircraft. The castle part was divided up into a reception area, kitchens and a variety of bedrooms on different confusing levels and up and down small stone stairways. The three concrete and glass wings contained most of the bedrooms and an auditorium, conference rooms and the vast dining room which was cantilevered out over the lake's edge.

'So as the Nazis withdrew,' Christopher was saying, 'the only organized force able to step in was the communists. But they'd been a military force, a partisan force, there was no *civil* organization. So inevitably there was great civil confusion. It was a sad period. The communist peasants went on the rampage. The churches, of course, took the brunt of it. Paintings, carvings, tapestries … so much of it smashed and put to the torch … so many beautiful things lost forever.'

He sighed.

'To them, of course,' he said, 'it was nothing but capitalist trumpery.'

Forde stopped and put his hand on Christopher's arm. He was overcome by a sudden warmth of feeling. With the earnestness and grave courtesy of the inebriated, Forde said, 'That is the first time in my life, Christopher, that I have heard the word "trumpery" used in conversation.'

'And you are the first person I have met,' said Christopher, 'to whom I could have said it *secure*,' raising his forefinger for emphasis, '*secure* in the knowledge it would be understood.'

They crunched on towards the hotel.

FORDE'S ROOM WAS IN THE WARREN of rooms in the castle part of the hotel. He had been in and out of it three times now since arriving at Splad that afternoon but was still uncertain of his route. He knew that he had to make a first turn left at the painting of the dead deer.

The corridors, staircases, and walled-in embrasures were hung with *nature morte de chasse* paintings. Early to mid-nineteenth century, most of them, he thought, though a few might have been earlier. It was a genre he'd always avoided, disliking the lavishing of such formidable technique on the depiction of wounds. There was something unsettling about the best of the paintings. He sensed in them a sexual relishing of cruelty and death. He felt repelled in the same way by what he thought of as the Mayan element in Mexican crucifixes, Christ's wounds shown to the white of the bone, shocking atavistic inlays of ivory.

He bent to peer at the small brass plate at the bottom of the frame but all it said was: 1831.

The deer was lying head down across a rustic bench. Two tensely seated hounds with mad eyes yearned up at it. In its nostrils, blood.

As he walked on down the silent corridor, he found himself groping for the name of Queen Victoria's favourite painter. The man whose animal paintings had got nastier and nastier, the cruelty coming closer to the surface, until his mind gave way entirely and he'd died years later barking mad. The man who did the lions at the foot of Nelson's monument in Trafalgar Square, the *Stag at Bay* man.

It was on the tip of his tongue

Began with 'L'.

Lutyens?

Battues of grouse and pheasants. A gralloched deer. Hecatombs of rabbits, grouse, partridges, snipe and ducks. In some of the paintings, for no obvious reason, greaves, helms, gorgets, a polished steel cuirass inlaid with brass, a drum bright with regimental crest and colours amid the piled, limp bodies.

He had to go up a short flight of stone steps just after a painting of a dead hawk and rabbit hanging upside down from a fence. Highlights glinted on the rabbit's eye and on the hawk's curved talons. The rabbit's grey fur was wind-ruffled to show the soft blue underfur pocked where pellets had struck, each swollen puncture dark with gore.

At the top of the steps he turned the wrong way. The short curving corridor terminated in a dead-end. He stood in the stone embrasure staring at the ice-making machine.

It rumbled and hummed.

'Landseer!' he exclaimed. 'Sir Edwin Landseer.'

He followed the corridor in the opposite direction and, recognizing the red brocade curtains partially drawn across the entrance to the recess, finally gained his room.

He felt relieved to lock his door. It had been a long day and he felt tired and crammed with undigested new experience. The bedroom had an antique look, the furniture old and heavy, the walls covered in some kind of grey material, slightly furry to the touch, velvet perhaps. Off the bedroom to the left was a bathroom and to the right a separate little room intended perhaps as a dressing room. It contained a chest of drawers and a long mirror in a gilt frame. He had been pleased to discover, in what had seemed to be a cupboard, a TV set and a mini-bar.

The thing Forde loathed most about travelling was *carrying things*. He hated lugging heavy cases about. He hated luggage itself. Luggage, he had often proposed to Sheila as she sat on her case to get it to close, reduced people to being its ill-tempered guardians. Who would wish to stand with the anxious herd watching tons of luggage tumbling onto carousels? Who would wish to share in that mesmerized silence as luggage trundled round and round?

Forde travelled only with a carry-on bag. He never carried more than two shirts, two pairs of underpants, and two pairs of socks. Sheila made up for him little Saran Wrap packages of Tide, each secured with a garbage bag tie and each sufficient to do one wash. Every night he washed his clothes in the washbasin, scrubbing clean the collars and cuffs of the shirts with an old toothbrush, and then hung everything over the bath to dry.

He lay in the dark letting his mind run back over the last two days to his landing in Ljubljana. Thought of his surprise at seeing booths at the airport for Avis and Hertz. At the taxi which accepted Visa and on whose tape deck the Stones were singing 'Midnight Rambler'. At the opulence of the Ljubljana

Holiday Inn. Hardly the grim face of Godless Communism he'd been looking forward to.

It had all been much like anywhere else.

He'd wandered the streets of the old city, the buildings distinguished but shabby, the river running through the centre of it all, graceful bridges, churches and nuns everywhere, the castle at the top of the hill boarded up because of the danger of falling masonry, no money, Christopher told him later, for renovation or repair.

But there was certainly money in the new part of the city. Most shop doors carried Visa and American Express stickers. Familiar names in windows – Black and Decker, Cuisinart, Braun. Parked along the streets, Audi, BMW, Volkswagen. In a bookstore window he'd seen translations of Jack Higgins, Wilbur Smith, Sidney Sheldon, Dick Francis and, to his mortification, an omnibus edition of three Jalna novels by Mazo de la Roche.

But the play of pictures in his mind kept going back to the taxi ride in from the airport. Woods. Small fields. Groups of men and women working in what he took to be allotments of some kind. A tethered donkey eating the roadside grass. In a vegetable garden, a woman working with a mattock.

Then a narrow stone humpback bridge, the road rising, and he'd been looking down over the side of the bridge into a meadow. And there he'd caught a flash of an enormous white bird standing.

He'd cried out to the driver to stop and back up. He'd pointed. The driver, rolling down his window and lighting a cigarette, said, 'You like such?'

He'd sat staring.

'What is it? What's it called?'

The driver said something, perhaps a name.

Mist hung over the stream. He could not see the water. The stream's course was plotted by polled willows. The bird was taller than the three grey stacked bales of last year's hay.

He guessed it stood nearly four feet high.

'Cranes,' Christopher had said on the bus from Ljubljana. 'I've somehow never really *warmed* to birds.'

'Not storks?'

'No, these are rather famous. They'll have been here for about two weeks now. They spend the winters in North Africa. Morocco, somewhere like that.'

'And they nest here? In Slovenia?'

'And always in the same place. They just pile new stuff on top of the old.'

'You mean the same birds go back to the same nest?'

'They mate for life, apparently. Some pairs have been together for fifty years.'

He pulled a face.

'Not really my cup of tea.'

As he slipped towards sleep just conscious of the irregular dripping sounds from his shirt in the bathroom, he imagined himself in the meadow trying to get closer to the crane without frightening it. The bird was aware of him and walked away keeping the distance between them constant. It walked slowly and gracefully, sometimes hesitating before setting down a foot, reminding him of the way herons stalk. He could see it quite clearly. Its body was white except for the bustle of tail feathers about its rump which were grey shading to black. Its long neck was black with a white patch around the eyes and on top of its head a cap of brilliant red. He edged closer. The crane was pacing along the margin of the mist, from time to time stopping and turning its head to the side as if listening. Past the old bales of hay and the field becoming squelchy, breaking down into tussocks and clumps. And as he looks up again from the unsure footing, the crane is stepping into the mist which accepts it and wreathes around it, hiding it from view.

THREE WAITERS IN MAUVE JACKETS and mauve bow ties
stood beside the buffet tables impassively surveying the
breakfasters. Their function seemed to be to keep the tables
stocked and tidy. From time to time they flapped their
napkins at crumbs. Two of them had luxuriant drooping
mustachios, growths he thought of as Serbian.

He inspected the array of dishes. Cornflakes, muesli,
pickled mushrooms, sliced ham, salami, liverwurst,
hardboiled eggs, smoked fish, triangles of processed Swiss
cheese in silver foil, a soft white cheese in liquid – either feta
or brinza – and small round cheeses covered in yellow wax
which he suspected might be kashkaval – honey, rolls, butter.
Juice in jugs. Milk. Coffee in thermos flasks.

No sign of Christopher so he took his tray to an uncrowded
table and nodded to a darkly Arab-looking man who
promptly passed him a card which read: Abdul-Rahman
Majeed Al-Mansoor. Baghdad. Iraq.

'Hello,' said Abdul-Rahman. 'How are you? I am fine.'

As Forde started to crack and peel shell from his egg, the
other man at the table took out his wallet and extracted a
card, saying, 'I hope that my coughing will not discommode
you. I cannot suppress it as the cough is hysterical in origin.
My card. Dorscht. Vienna. Canadianist.'

Pretending abstraction, Forde busied himself with his
breakfast. Covertly he watched Dorscht. Dorscht had a black
plastic thermos jug from which he was pouring ... hot water.
He was wearing a leather purse or pouch on a strap which
crossed his chest. The archaic word 'scrip' flashed into Forde's
mind. From his purse Dorscht took a cracker, a Ryvita-
looking thing, and started nibbling.

The hubbub in the room was rising to a constant roar.
Three men and two women brought trays to the table. They
seemed to be a mixture of Canadians and Americans and all
seemed to know each other. They were arguing about a poet.

'... but surely he's *noted* for his deconstruction of binaries.'

'... and by the introduction of chorus avoids the monological egocentricity of conventional lyric discourse.'

Christ!

'Let me say,' brayed one of the men, 'let me say, in full awareness of heteroglossia ...'

Christ!

Dorscht performed his chugging cough.

Abdul-Rahman Majeed Al-Mansoor belched and patted prissily at his lips with a paper napkin.

Dorscht had a little silver box now which he evidently kept with his crackers. He was selecting from it three kinds of pills. One of them looked like Valium.

Suddenly Forde sensed someone close to him, was aware someone was staring at him. He turned his head and looked up.

Her arm was raised as though she'd been about to touch his shoulder.

'It *is* ... isn't it?' she said.

'Yes.'

He got to his feet.

'I'm so happy,' she said.

'Karla,' he said.

AT THE NARROW END OF THE LAKE the water was shallow and choked with weed. The air was rank with the smell of mud and rotting vegetation. Karla stopped and pointed down into the water.

'What is the name of this in English?'

Floating there just a foot from the edge of the lake was a mass of frog spawn. He knelt on one knee and worked his hands under the jelly, raising it slightly. It was the size of a soccer ball. He was amazed at the weight of the mass, amazed and then suddenly not amazed, pierced by memory, transported back to his ten-year-old self. He saw himself crouching beside a pool in an abandoned gravel pit which was posted with signs saying DANGER. NO TRESPASSING. On the ground beside him stood his big Ovaltine jar with air holes punched through the lid. It was full of frog spawn. He was catching palmated newts with a small net made of clumsily stitched lace curtain and placing them in his weed-filled tin. All about him yellow coltsfoot flowers.

'In German,' she said, 'you say *Froschlaich*.'

Some of the intensely black dots were already starting to elongate into commas. As she bent to look, her hair touched his cheek. The mass of jelly poured out of his hands and slipped back into the water sinking and then rising again to ride just beneath the surface.

Forde felt almost giddy. His hands were tingling from the coldness of the water. He felt obscurely excited by the memory the feel of the frog spawn had prompted. He felt he could not breathe in deeply enough. The sun was hot on his back. After months of grinding winter it was a joy not to be wearing boots, a joy not to be wearing a parka, a joy to see the lime-green leaves, the froth of foliage, to hear bird song, sunlight hinting and glinting on the water, dandelions glowing, growing from crevices in the rock face the delicate fronds of hart's-tongue ferns.

He wanted to hold this place and moment in his mind forever.

Ahead of them a café bright with umbrellas. They sat at a patio table and drank cappuccinos, the lake's soft swell lapping at the patio's wooden pilings. Everything conspired to please, the sun, the water sounds, the stiffness of the foam on his coffee, the crisp paper wrapping on the sugar cubes. He watched her hands, the glint of transparent varnish on her fingernails.

Into a sudden silence, Forde said, 'And ... ah ... Viktor?'

She raised an eyebrow.

'I suppose Viktor's with your husband.'

'Oh, no,' she said. 'He's staying with a friend of mine from the university. He likes it there. She spoils him and she has a hound he can play with.'

'Hmmm,' said Forde.

'And he knows that when I return I will be bringing presents.'

Forde nodded.

They walked on to finish the circuit of the lake. As they neared the hotel, Karla said, 'Tell me about your name. I've often wondered about this. In English, people who are Robert are called Bob. So are you called Bob or Robert?'

'Well, sometimes Rob but the people closest to me seem to call me Forde.'

She paused in the doorway.

'Then I, too,' she declared, 'will address you as Forde.'

He sketched a comic caricature of a Germanic bow.

'My colleagues will be wondering where I am,' she said. 'I must go and hear a paper.'

'We'll meet for dinner?'

She smiled and nodded.

'But I must change my shoes.'

She put her hand on his arm and then turned and walked off across the hotel lobby.

He looked into the dining room in hopes of finding Christopher but the buffet tables had been stacked away and a lone waiter was droning away with vacuum cleaner.

Papers were being delivered in all the conference rooms. He eased open doors.

'... his fiction is sociolect and foregrounds the process of enunciation.'

Christ!

'... the analytico-referential discourse reinstalls itself covering up a self-referential critique which ...'

Christ!

In the small bar just off the lobby he settled himself with a bottle of Becks and, writing on the blank pages of an

36

abandoned conference programme, started to make notes. The feel of the frog spawn had unsettled him. He was startled by the intensity of the images and the spate of words he was dashing onto the pages. He had no idea what he might use it for, but he certainly wasn't going to question the gift.

Around the top of the old gravel pit bramble bushes grew in profusion. In late August and early September they were heavy with blackberries. He used the curved handle of a walking stick to draw the laden shoots towards him. He always took the blackberries to his grandmother who made blackberry and apple pies and blackberry vinegar to pour on pancakes.

His maternal grandparents lived in a tiny, jerry-built, company-owned row house not many miles from the pit where his grandfather had worked all his life. The backs of the houses looked onto a squalid cobbled square where vivid algae slimed the open drains. In the centre of the square stood a row of outhouses and a communal stand pipe. Surrounding the square were tumbledown sheds in which were kept gardening tools, work benches, rabbits, old bicycles, junk. And towering above the houses and the yard up on the hillside stood an abandoned factory.

The factory was a classic Victorian building of iron and glass. Had someone told him once it had been a shoe factory? Every time he had gone out of the back door, there it was, derelict, looming dark over the yard. Many of the glass panels were shattered or gaped blank. The road that ran up to the front of it was disused and closed off by an iron gate hung with threatening notices. Brambles and nettles grew right up to the walls. The building both lured and frightened him. It was a place of mystery. His mother and his grandparents had told him constantly of its danger.

'You go there,' his grandfather cackled, 'and the tramps'll get you.'

Falling glass. Rotting boards. Trespass.

The pencil racing.

He bore in on it.

(Why machinery not melted down in 1939 for munitions?)

Inside – very quiet, *still*. The floor loud with glass. The
light is dim – gloomy – subaqueous. Yes. Factory like sunken
ship. Silt and weed have blunted its shape. The machinery is
actually *changing shape*. What was once precise geometry –
straight lines of steel – is now blurring, becoming *rounded* by
rust and decay. Furred. Dali. Pigeon shit growing like guano.
Whitewash on walls leprous and swollen. Brutality of the
shapes and spaces oppressive. Girders, I-beams – name of
place Nazis hanged Bomb Plot people with piano wire? Check.
Spaces have that kind of feel.

What is going to happen here?

'THERE'S KARLA ON THE LEFT,' Forde said to Christopher.

They watched the three women coming across the lobby.

'Which do you think's the heavy?' said Christopher.

'What do you mean?'

'The minder.'

'*What?*'

'Oh, really, Robert,' said Christopher. 'Don't be *impossibly*
naive.'

The other two women went into the dining room.

'Karla,' said Forde, 'may I introduce you to Christopher
Harris. Karla Schiff.'

'Enchanted,' said Christopher in a flat tone.

But the menu cheered him up. It was written in Slovene
and English. It offered: Ham Dumplings with Fried Potatoes,
Veal Ribs with Fried Potatoes, and Butter Pies with Chicken
Pluck.

'That *is* rather good, isn't it?' said Christopher. 'The
Slovene would suggest they mean what Americans call
"chicken pot pie".'

The din was extraordinary and as wine bottles appeared was getting louder. Waiters and waitresses were carrying plates on the largest trays Forde had ever seen. They must have been four feet across. The waitresses were wearing what he thought of as Roman-legionnaire sandals, straps wound up round the ankles and shin. Karla's shoes were made of plaited brown leather and were narrow and elegant and seemed to him very expensive-looking. He still felt slightly dissociated, still a little dazed by that world of memory and imagination, and was content to watch Karla and let rain down upon him the sparks and boom and brilliance of Christopher's performance.

Slovene wine production understandably collective rather than *Mis en Bouteilles au Château* so the height of praise would perhaps be the word *serviceable....*

Forde smiled and sipped.

Karla was wearing a loose white muslin blouse whose changing configurations kept his eye returning.

He wondered where Dorscht was seated; he sensed that Dorscht had immense possibilities.

He suddenly noticed that Christopher had tended to his nose with pancake make-up.

Frescos again. Mid-fourteenth century. The death of John the Baptist. A tiny perfect chapel near Bohinj. The headless corpse gouting blood in three streams. Angels decorated the other walls. One angel had a triple goitre.

'If only Bernard Berenson had visited Slovenia,' Christopher said, 'our frescos would be famous throughout the world.'

'The Master of Bohinj,' said Forde.

'The Master of the Goitre,' said Christopher.

'Master of the Goitred Angel,' said Forde.

'*Amico*,' said Christopher, 'of the Master of the Goitred Angel.'

Forde laughed delightedly.

'It isn't kind, Forde,' said Karla, 'it isn't being nice to talk at dinner about things I don't understand.'

Her lips moved into the faintest suggestion of a pout and Forde was enchanted.

AS HE SLUICED HIS SHIRT IN THE WASHBASIN, he burped and the taste of tarragon cake revisited him. They had gone to the bar off the lobby after dinner and had drunk something Christopher claimed was a local specialty, a pear brandy, but it hadn't tasted of pears and was aggressively nasty like grappa or marc and the bar had been cramped and jammed with people talking about the materiality of the signifier.

Forde was beginning to feel rather peculiar. He felt hot and somehow bloated though he had not eaten much of the ham dumplings. The fluorescent lights in the bathroom were unusually harsh and turned the white tiles, chrome and red rubber mat into a restraining room in a hospital for the criminally insane. He studied his face in the mirror. When he swallowed, his throat seemed constricted. He wondered if he was getting a cold.

He decided that he might ward it off by taking vitamin C and an extra aspirin. He took an aspirin every day to thin his blood. The heart attack that was going to fell him was never far from his conscious thought. He decided that if he took vitamin C with a Scotch from the mini-bar and added to the Scotch a little *warm* water, this would render the Scotch medicinal, but the drink burned and it felt as if he were pouring alcohol onto raw flesh. He had difficulty swallowing the pills.

He went back into the bathroom and took off his underpants to wash them and thought how very silly men looked naked but for socks. Pain was clutching his stomach. He sat on the toilet in the mad light emitting high-pitched keening farts which culminated in an explosive discharge. He stood and looked in the toilet and then bent and peered. Finally, he knelt to look. Floating on the surface were three whitish things each ringed with what looked like froth. They looked exactly like the water-steeped jasmine flowers in Chinese tea.

Florets, he thought.

An efflorescence in his bowels.

Benign?

Or cancerous?

Despite the aspirin, he still felt hot, feverish. He switched on the bedside lamp. He lay naked on top of the coverlet. The grey velvet on the walls was dappled with faded spots which showed in this light like the subtle rosettes on a black leopard's flanks.

He switched the light off and lay in the dark, feeling ill and swallowing with difficulty. His head was aching. The room felt close about him, furry. He seemed to sense the grey walls almost imperceptibly moving as if they were breathing. He slept fitfully, dozing, waking with a start, drifting off deeper to lose himself in a chaotic and terrifying dream, the narrow beam of his flashlight cutting into the darkness, a trussed body hanging from a steel beam, the broken glass loud under his feet.

ON TOP OF THE CLIFF which rose at the head of the lake stood another small castle. According to Christopher, it had been extensively altered in the eighteenth century to turn it into something more comfortable, more domestic. The Nazis had used it as a recreation centre for army officers. Now it had been turned into a museum which housed an absolutely undistinguished collection of artifacts. Drinks and snacks were served on the ramparts.

It was possible to climb up the cliff on a wandering trail through the trees and then scramble the last fifty yards or so on scree and skirt the parapet to come at a side gate.

Forde turned back and watched Karla scrambling up

below him. As she reached the steepest pitch, he leaned down and extended his hand. She looked up at him, winded, a smudge of hair stuck to her forehead with sweat. She reached up and grasped his hand and he took the weight of her and pulled her up over the last of the scree onto the track below the wall.

The museum delighted him. It was exactly like one-room museums in provincial English towns, haphazard accumulations of local finds, curios brought home by colonial officers, the last resting place of the hobbies of deceased gentry.

They browsed over the glass cases of unidentified pottery shards, stone hand axes, arrowheads, bronze fibulae, plaster casts of Roman and Greek coins, powder flasks of polished horn, bullet moulds, bowls heaped with thirteenth-century coins of Béla IV of Hungary, fossils, Roman perfume bottles, stilettos, poniards, medieval tiles with slip decoration the colour of humbugs.

Forde stopped and exclaimed and bent over a display case.

'What is it?' said Karla.

'Look how pretty!' he said.

Forde stared at the leather object. He had never seen one before. The leather was rigid rather than pliable. It was a leather tube which flared like a champagne cork at the open end. Three quarters of the way up, the tube bent over like a cowl and tapered slightly to a close. The stitching was precise and delicate, the leather dark with age, glossy, and chased with a wreathing convolvulus design. The whole thing was about the size of a shuttlecock.

'It *has* to be,' said Forde. 'It's a hood for a falcon.'

He was moved by the craftsmanship, by the thought of the hands that had gentled the hood over a hawk's head, by the sudden opening into the past the hood afforded.

'I'd love to touch that,' he said. 'I'd love to hold that in my hands.'

He tried the case but it was locked.

42

When they'd exhausted the possibilities of the museum, they wandered out into the garden and then climbed to the ramparts and sat under an umbrella, sipping lemonade through straws. The length of the lake lay silver before them, the hotel, the marina, ex-King Peter's summer palace. A small yacht was tacking up towards them.

'You see, Karla,' he suddenly burst out, '*that's* where art comes from. That leather hood. It arises from the realness of the world. Of course, art encompasses ideas but it's not *about* ideas. It's more concerned with feeling. And you capture the feeling through things, through particularity. There's nothing *intellectual* about novels.'

Suddenly embarrassed, he busied himself with lemonade and straw.

Karla was reading his face.

They strolled back towards the hotel, following the road which led gently downhill all the way. Forde, still ravished by greenness, growth, the lemon-green of leaves, stopped to pick some wild flowers. He presented the bouquet to Karla. Daisies, white cow parsley, purple vetch, and campion both pink and white.

THE VENISON WAS TOUGH AND FIBROUS. It was accompanied by a compote of red berries. Nobody knew what they were called but Professor Dorscht thought that in English they might possibly be called cloudberries. Though he could in no way guarantee that that was so.

Forde had been studying the programme earlier and said to Dorscht, 'So tomorrow's the day of your paper.'

Dorscht inclined his head.

'About Lucy Maud Montgomery, isn't it?'

'Lucy *who?*' warbled Christopher.

'Specifically,' said Dorscht, 'the Emily novels.'

'Emily?' repeated Forde.

'They are lesser-known works of her maturity.'

Works, thought Forde, who considered it something of a national embarrassment that Canadian scholars and universities studied the output of a hack writer of children's books.

'This is another Canadian writer I do not know about it,' said Karla. 'There is so much for a Canadianist to learn.'

'Oh, not really,' said Forde who was tempted to express the opinion that the best Canadian writing could be accommodated on a three-foot shelf.

Christopher was beginning to slur his words.

'Lucy *who?*' he said again investing the word 'who' with patent incredulity.

'What I term the "Emily" novels,' said Dorscht, 'is the trilogy of novels beginning in 1923 with *Emily of New Moon* and followed in 1925 by *Emily Climbs* and concluding in 1927 with *Emily's Quest*. My paper will – I think the most appropriate word is "probe" – my paper will probe the trilogy's mythic aspects.'

Mythic scrotums, thought Forde. *Mythic bollocks*.

Forde watched Dorscht peel his apple with a little silver penknife. His ability to digest was limited, he had explained, his health undermined by the tensions generated during the long years of study leading to his doctorate, years made unendurable by the psychological savagery visited upon him by his supervising professor.

'But what I mean *is*,' insisted Christopher, 'who *is* she?'

'*So*, Robert Forde!' boomed a familiar voice.

He automatically started to get to his feet, but a heavy hand on his shoulder rammed him down again into his seat.

'May I introduce,' he said generally, 'Drago Tomović.'

'And who,' said Drago, 'is this most *beauteous* lady?'

He smiled a gold-toothed smile that was revoltingly roguish.

'Drago has translated my novel *Winter Creatures* into Serbian.'

Drago with mock flourish handed a package across the table. Forde tore open the paper.

It was in Cyrillic.

It had no cover art.

The paper was hairy.

Karla suggested they celebrate the translation in the bar off the lobby. The evening wore on. Drago's flappy jacket was in huge checks like the outrageous clothes worn by comedians in vaudeville or music hall. Christopher made it quite clear by grimace and the stiffness of his body that he found Drago appalling. Dorscht could not drink alcohol because of his ulcer. He also confided that he feared losing control. Drago flirted ponderously with Karla. Christopher started to read the translation making loud tut and click noises.

Through the surf of conversation Forde kept overhearing snatches of astounding drivel from a bony woman behind him who was, apparently, uncovering a female language by decoding patriarchal deformation.

Christ!

'Winter,' boomed Drago, 'is not just *winter*.' He tapped his forehead. '*Think!* It *stands for* the coldness between the characters. Always say to yourself what is the *hidden* meaning of this book. Andrew is not *just* a bureaucrat. He works for the *government* and so *represents* …'

'You mean,' said Karla, 'that you read the book as …' She groped for the word. '… as an allegory?'

'*Certainly*,' said Drago.

Forde was horrified.

'I make everything,' said Drago, '*crystal clear*.'

Dorscht went into another coughing fit.

When he'd finished and done the tic-thing with his left eye, Forde pressed him for details of the psychological savagery visited upon him by his supervising professor. Dorscht revealed that he had been commanded to write papers which his professor then appropriated and delivered at conferences as his own work. That the professor would only discuss his thesis in expensive restaurants where Dorscht was always forced to pay the bill. That for years he had to take the professor's clothes to the laundry and dry-cleaners and then deliver them to the man's house.

Christopher interrupted Dorscht's lamentations by slapping shut *Winter Creatures* and walking round the table to hand it to Forde, saying, 'Oaf and boor.'

To Dorscht, Karla and Drago, he said, 'I am now going to bed.'

His leaving broke the party up. Dorscht went off to take a Valium and a mild barbiturate, Drago was swept up in the lobby by a noisy group of fellow Serbians who were all wearing what Forde took to be the rosettes and coloured favours of a soccer team, and Karla was claimed just outside the doors of the bar by her two friends from Jena.

She turned to look back at him; she smiled and shrugged.

Forde made his way up past the deer with blood in its nostrils, climbed the stairs at the pellet-pocked rabbit and the hawk with the shattered wing. His room felt stuffy and hot. He flipped through the translation of *Winter Creatures* but the only thing he could read was his name. But even if Drago had reduced a sprightly comedy to a stodgy allegory of his own invention, a book was still a book and it had his name on it. And if one thought of the Cyrillic as a kind of abstract art, the pages were not unattractive.

He filled the sink in the bathroom and poured in one of Sheila's Saran Wrap packages of Tide. He took off his clothes and immersed the shirt pushing it down repeatedly to get the air pockets out. He was beginning to feel decidedly odd again. A band of constriction across his forehead. Difficulty swallowing. He wondered if there was something about the room itself. Outside it, he felt entirely normal. Perhaps he was allergic to something in the room. Though he'd never suffered from allergies before. And the first night he'd slept in the room had been uneventful.

His mouth kept filling with saliva as if at any moment he might vomit. Perhaps they were using some devastating East European or Balkan chemical to clean the carpets or the bath.

He felt not only hot but distressed and confused by his discomfort. He wandered into the bedroom and sat in the armchair hoping that if he concentrated on reading he would be able to ignore or conquer the symptoms. He always travelled with a copy of *Hart's Rules for Compositors and Readers at the University Press Oxford* because it was small and inexhaustible. But the print swam and he kept putting the book down and staring at the furry wall, concentrating on not throwing up.

The venison?

But no one else had seemed affected.

And didn't it take twelve hours or more to incubate or whatever one called it?

He forced himself back into the bathroom and scrubbed the shirt's collar and cuffs with the old toothbrush. He rinsed the shirt in the bathtub, leaving the soapy water in the basin to do his underpants and socks.

He sat on the toilet but nothing resulted. The fluorescent lights hummed. He thought suddenly of an eccentric landlady he'd once had when he was at university. She'd been having the house painted and had walked in on one of the painters who was on the toilet. In great embarrassment he'd said to her that he was having a pee.

'What kind of a man,' she'd demanded, 'sits down to squeeze his lemons?'

Why had *that* swum into his mind?

He lay on the bed and tried to sleep but under the covers he was too hot, on top of them too cold. The nausea had settled into uneasiness in his stomach and at the back of his throat. Pictures churned about in his mind. Karla looking up at him from the steep scree. The falcon's hood delicate and as light on the palm, he imagined, as a blown bird's egg. In the gilt cabinet, the plaited silk jesses with silver varvels. The roadside flowers. Pink and white campion.

He felt small cramps of pain in his stomach. He flung back the covers again and went to sit on the toilet. He strained briefly but nothing happened. He got up and realized immediately that something *had* happened. The toilet bowl was speckled with a fine mist of blood. Through the toilet paper his incredulous fingertips felt a lump, a lump with three – his fingertips explored that heat and hugeness – a vast lump with three.... What *was* this? A Pile? Piles? What *were* piles? Exactly? Such a thing had never happened to him before. His fingertips traced the dimensions and configurations of the horror. A lump with three ... *lobes.*

The very word filled his mouth with clear saliva.

His hand smelled and was sticky with watery blood.

He twisted round trying to look at his behind in the mirror.

He put one foot on the toilet seat and bent forward separating his cheeks, but this position revealed nothing but redness.

A woman had once told him that after giving birth she'd had piles 'like a bunch of grapes'.

He waddled across the bedroom into the dressing room with its full-length mirror and contorted himself variously and ingeniously but could see nothing. He imagined it to be blue or purple. He didn't want to get too yogic in his postures in case the horror burst.

He began to feel panicky. He could not endure the embarrassment of requesting treatment. But he did not wish to leak to death in a Slovenian hotel. He made a pad of a dozen or so Kleenex and wedged it between his cheeks and over the thing. He eased on clean underpants to keep the pad in place. Then he put on a clean shirt and his trousers and taking his key and the plastic ice-bucket set off down the corridor with tiny steps towards the ice machine.

Back in the bathroom he leaned his weary head on his arm

48

on the vanity and with his right hand held ice cube after ice cube against the hot swollen lumps his body had extruded, ice water trickling down his legs into his toes, his scrotum frozen, fingers numb even through the flannel, weary, weary for his bed.

FORDE WAS SITTING WITH KARLA. Christopher was sitting in the seat behind. The bus, one of four, was taking the conference people on this final day for a picnic in a village high up near Mt. Triglav in the Julian Alps.

Forde was feeling cheerful and restored. His piles had retreated entirely. His reading and lecture the day before had been well attended. Even Forde had been surprised by how rude he had been to an earnest man at the lecture who had put a question to him which had involved the name 'Bakhtin' and the words 'dialogic', 'foregrounded', and 'problematized'. Though he felt absolutely no contrition. That night he had again felt ill and feverish but suffered nothing worse than a rash over his torso and thighs, hot white welts that itched and throbbed and bled when scratched. He had tried to soothe the itching by repeatedly applying a flannel soaked in ice-water.

He was sure he was suffering from an allergy either to something in the room or to food.

He had read from his last novel, *Tincture of Opium*. He'd done a restaurant scene involving the two lovers and a Chinese waiter who understood little English and whose every utterance sounded like a barked command. It was a set-piece but it performed well, modulating from near-farce to a delicate affirmation of love. He particularly liked the way he'd cut the sweetness of the sentiment with comic intrusions.

At dinner that night Karla had arranged with the Oliver Hardy waiter for a bottle of champagne to be brought to their table. She had proposed a toast to Forde's wonderful reading, to his glittering novels, to his eminence in Canadian letters, to his generosity with his time to beginning Canadianists, to, well, *Forde!*

She had been flushed, her eyes shining.

'Bottoms up!' cried Christopher.

'Sincere felicitations,' said Professor Dorscht.

'To Forde!' said Karla again.

'*Certainly* to Forde!' boomed Drago.

Now he could feel her thigh swayed warm against his as the bus made turn after turn climbing the narrow road terraced into the mountain. The buses parked outside the boundary of the Triglav National Park, and people set out to walk the mile or so through woods and meadows to the village. The sun was pleasantly warm, the surrounding mountains serenely beautiful. The mountains enclosed them, cupped them. It was, thought Forde, rather like being on the stage of a vast amphitheatre. In places, the path they were walking along ran over outcroppings of rock. They stopped to help an elderly couple whose leather-soled shoes were slipping on the smoothed stone.

'What are those wooden things?' asked Forde.

'They're racks for drying hay on,' said Christopher. 'Unique to Slovenia. They're called *kozolci*.'

'And look!' said Forde. 'Cowslips and primroses. I haven't seen those for years.'

'And here,' said Christopher, 'are some of our famous gentians.'

Forde stopped. He stared down at the intensity of the blue.

'Oh, yes,' said Karla. 'In German we say *Enzian*.'

'This is a very special day for me,' said Forde. He got down on his knees and brushed the grass aside. 'I've never seen a gentian before. I read about them when I was in my teens. I used to learn poems off by heart that I liked the sound of and there was one called "Bavarian Gentians" by D. H. Lawrence.

Well, perhaps it's not such a good poem. Perhaps you're extra forgiving to things you liked when you were young '
	He looked up at Karla.
	He frowned slightly in concentration.

Reach me a gentian, give me a torch!
let me guide myself with the blue, forked torch of this flower
down the darker and darker stairs, where blue is darkened on
	blueness
even where Persephone goes, just now, from the frosted September
to the sightless realm where darkness is awake upon the dark
and Persephone herself is but a voice
or a darkness invisible enfolded in the deeper dark
of the arms Plutonic, and pieced with the passion of dense gloom,
among the splendour of torches of darkness, shedding darkness on
	the lost bride and her groom.

	'Stone the crows!' said Christopher. 'Do you do that often?'
	'No,' said Forde. 'It's weird. Only with things I learned when I was about sixteen.'
	'Sort of idiot savant-ish,' said Christopher.
	'It *sounds* beautiful,' said Karla.
	'Well,' said Forde, getting up and brushing wisps of dry grass off his trousers, 'sometimes I think it's nothing *but* sound but then the old bastard gets off things like "darkness is awake upon the dark" and you have to admit …'
	The path through the meadow joined a wider path that led down into the village. A large banner was strung across the path. On it were the words:
	WELCOME TO THE CULTURAL WORKERS.
	The straggling procession from the buses was beginning to pool now around the village hall where rustic tables and benches were set out. The villagers were greeting each newcomer with trays of bread and salt and shot glasses of slivovitz. The men were in Alpine costume, long tight white

pants, thigh-high black leather boots, embroidered waistcoats. Cummerbund things. Or lederhosen. The women wore layered skirts and waistcoats and bonnets. Forde found it oddly unreal. Slightly embarrassing. He felt it was like being on the set of a Hollywood musical.

Some of the men were carrying crates of beer and cases of wine from the village hall and setting up one of the tables as a bar.

'The best beer,' said Christopher, 'is this Gambrinus. And Union's quite good, too. They brew that in Ljubljana. And for wine, I'd stick to Refošk or Kraški Teran.'

'Who's paying for all this?'

'The Literary and Cultural Association of Slovenia and the local Party boss.'

'And what about ...'

'The peasants?' said Christopher.

'I wish you wouldn't keep saying that.'

'Why?' said Christopher. 'Peasants are a recognizable class. In France, Germany, Italy, Spain ... *everywhere*. Peasants are peasants.'

'Oh, *very* much in Austria and Bavaria,' said Karla.

On the concrete slab in front of the village hall three young men were setting up amplifiers and speakers and going in and out of the hall trailing wire. Lying on and propped against the kitchen chairs were a bass, two guitars, and an amplified zither. Another man arrived and started messing about with a snare drum.

A little girl of about four or five dressed in skirts and bonnet was wandering through the tables staring at the people. She clutched to her chest an enormous and uncomfortable-looking rabbit.

The drummer's peremptory rattings and tattings and paradiddles sounded through the roar of conversation. Two of the village women were spreading white linen tablecloths over three of the tables. As they flipped the cloths in the air, they flashed like white sails against the vast blueness, a sky so huge that it made him think of the word 'empyrean'. The warmth of the sun, the azure sky, the stillness of the mountains all around – a sigh of pleasure escaped him. Dishes, bowls, pans, and platters began coming out of the village hall. They strolled over to look. Fried pork. Sausages with sauerkraut. Pork crackling. Fried veal with mushrooms. Pork hocks. Beans and chunks of veal in tomato sauce. Pasta stuffed with cottage cheese. Hunks of bread in baskets.

'That's the only thing to avoid,' said Christopher, pointing. 'It's a sort of cheese pie called *burek* and it's *terminally* greasy.'

They filled paper plates and Christopher exchanged pleasantries with the man behind the bar and snagged a bottle of Refošk.

The band started to play polkas and waltzes. An accordion came to join them. The music was just the thing for a picnic in the Alps, jolly and silly. Forde drank more wine and found himself tapping his foot in time to the rattletrap drummer.

He noticed some of the village men raising their hats to a man who had just arrived. He was wearing a black suit and a black shirt with a priest's white collar. But on his head was a bowler hat with pheasant feathers pinned to one side of it to form a tall, swaying cockade. He made his way through the villagers, shaking hands and slapping backs until he reached the bar where he was immediately handed not a shot glass but a tumbler of slivovitz. Forde had known some gargantuan drinkers in his day but he had never before seen a man *purple* with drink.

'He is both notorious and widely loved,' said Christopher. 'Later on – he always does – he'll sing a selection of sentimental and dirty songs.'

When they'd finished eating, Forde volunteered to fetch beer. The slow beer line-up brought him alongside a table of cultural workers who, seemingly oblivious to meadows or mountains, were locked in earnest discussion. As he stood there he heard a man say 'univocal discourse'. He looked with loathing upon these money-changers in the temple.

As he put the three bottles of Gambrinus down on the table, Christopher was saying, 'Well, the high point of the day for me is the absence of that hulking *Serb*.'

'Drago is not my fault,' said Forde.

'He certainly isn't mine.'

'*Certainly!*' said Forde. '*Certainly!*'

The crowd around the food tables was thinning out. Some of the conference people had drifted away higher in the meadow and were lying down sunbathing. The band had returned after a break and was playing waltzes. Forde had had enough to drink for the day to feel dreamlike and desultory. Some couples were waltzing in the village street. Forde idly watched the swirl of skirts. The sun was getting hotter. He started to peel the label off his beer bottle.

Karla got up and, pointing down the street, said, 'Forde! Take me dancing.'

He looked up at her.

He hesitated.

'Karla,' he said. 'I have eaten sausage and sauerkraut. Fried potatoes. Fried mushrooms. And that sheep cheese. I must have drunk a bottle of wine. And beer. I *might*,' he said, 'just might be able to manage a slow stroll in the meadows.'

People started to crowd around the band.

'Must be Father Baraga,' said Christopher.

They walked over and joined the crowd. Father Baraga was sitting on a wooden kitchen chair, hands on his thighs, beaming and purple. The zither man was lowering and adjusting the microphone. The musicians conferred with Father Baraga and a song was agreed upon.

It was obviously a kind of patter song, and the priest accompanied it with exaggerated facial expressions indicative of leering surprise, outrage, shock. Everyone who understood Slovene was laughing and grinning.

'What's it about?'

'Oh, this is a mild one,' said Christopher. 'It's all innuendo and *double entendre*. Like old music hall songs.' He thought for a second. 'You know –

"In the spring, my Auntie Nellie,
Dusting down her Botticelli"

– that sort of thing.'

Watching the rubbery lips, the sweat running from the bags under his eyes, the spittle, the purple flesh bulging onto the white collar, the yellow stumps of his teeth, Forde felt again how dreamlike, even nightmarish, the world so often seemed.

His novels were often criticized for containing what reviewers and critics described as 'grotesques' and 'caricatures'. What world, he wondered, did they live in? They carped and belly-ached that some of his scenes were 'improbable' or 'strained credulity' yet Forde knew that this was the way the world *was*. The world was bizarre. The word 'normal' was simply a notion.

He shrugged as he thought about it.

He was more than halfway up a very high mountain listening to a Fender bass being played by a man in thigh-length leather boots, to two guitars being played by men in lederhosen, to an amplified zither being played by another man in thigh-length leather boots, and to the singing of a drunken Roman Catholic priest wearing a bowler hat with feathers in it. *And* he was in the company of a woman Christopher had implied might well be a Stasi informer.

Karla caught his eye and motioned with her head. He followed her, working his way out of the crowd. They strolled up through the meadow, past the sunbathers, past hay racks, until they were high enough on the narrow trail to look down on the roof of the village hall. Karla was wearing her hair in a ponytail that bobbed as she walked. He thought of the photograph she'd sent. The photograph that was inside the calendar in his desk drawer. In that picture her hair had been short and helmet-shaped.

They could see only three houses on the main street with another set back from it by about fifty yards. Not that the street was really a street. It was just an unpaved, sandy path. The rest of the houses were dotted about the meadows. As they stood there, Forde was very aware of Karla's toenails. She had painted them a silvery colour.

The path they were walking along ran in front of three houses, grouped together. The house in the centre sported a frieze of stylized flowers painted just below the eaves. Outside the house stood the little girl in skirts and bonnet they'd seen earlier lugging her rabbit about.

The rabbit was lying in the grass unmoving except for one ear which turned to monitor its world. Karla smiled at the child and bent down to pet the rabbit.

'*Das ist doch ein hübscher Kerl!*'

The child laughed and swooped on the rabbit, hauling it up to her chest, its hind legs dangling. Just as Karla reached out to stroke it, the rabbit squirmed and raked the inside of her forearm with its back legs. She cried out in surprise. The little girl dropped the rabbit and squatted beside it and seemed to be scolding it. As Forde watched, blood welled into the two scratches, rose into large beads, ran.

'Animal things are always bad news,' said Forde. 'Dog bites, that sort of thing. They're always dirty. You probably ought to get a tetanus shot, but for now …'

He took her arm. He held her with his left hand just above her elbow. With his right hand he held her hand. He bent over the inside of her forearm. On her wrist he could smell the fragrance of Ysatis. He sucked the length of the two scratches, filling his mouth with blood and spitting it out onto the grass. Suck and spit. Suck and spit.

Karla laced her fingers with his.

HIS MOUTH TASTED VILE and he could hardly get his eyes open. He'd obviously slept for far longer than the nap he'd intended. His watch had stopped. He went into the bathroom and looked at his puffy face in the mad fluorescence. He'd caught the sun.

He went down to the dining room. The lobby was deserted. He heaved open the door to the dining room. The vast room was empty and silent. The chandeliers blazed light on the emptiness. By the trestle tables used as a service station, two of the waiters were silently folding a tablecloth. Arms raised above their heads, the corners of the cloth held between thumb and forefingers, they advanced upon each other. The corners met. The fat waiter stooped and picked up the bottom edge. He retreated until the cloth was taut then advanced again to meet and make a second fold. They looked as if they were performing an elephantine parody of a courtly dance.

The door thunked shut behind him.

He went into the bar off the lobby. There were three people there. He supposed some of the conference people had already left. He discovered that it was nearly nine-thirty. The buses had arrived back at Splad at about six-thirty so he'd been asleep for nearly three hours. He wound his watch and reset it.

He wondered if he ought to call Karla or Christopher.

He stood in the silent lobby in indecision.

Then he turned and started up the stairs, left at the deer, up the stone steps at the rabbit and hawk, hardly noticing them now they were familiar. He felt quite groggy from the unexpectedly deep sleep. He sat in the armchair in the bedroom and immediately started to feel even worse. His mouth was filling with saliva. He was feeling waves of nausea. He mastered the surge of vomit long enough to get into the bathroom where he vomited copiously and uncontrollably. He braced himself with both hands against the wall and stood, head hanging over the toilet bowl, breathing through open mouth, drooling, strings of saliva and mucus glistening from his lower lip. His stomach seized again and again and he vomited until he was vomiting nothing but bile and his throat was raw. He was in a cold sweat and his legs were trembling. He could feel the sweat cold on his ribs.

When the nausea faded, he brushed his teeth and cleaned the rim of the toilet and the underside of the spattered toilet seat. As he was doing so, he realized that something was happening to his vision. Bright white sparks seemed to be drifting across things, the sensation intensifying until there was a gauze obscuring things like the snow of interference on a TV screen. He felt quite frightened and went back into the bedroom feeling his way along the walls. He got himself onto the bed and lay there wondering what was happening to him, what he ought to do.

He opened his eyes again, but the silent crackle of white dots still veiled the bedside lamp, the occasional table, the bed itself. He closed his eyes and tried to think calmly about his situation. Were the vomiting and the white dots related? Could they have the same cause? Why might he have vomited? Wine? Extremely unlikely. Might he be suffering from sunstroke? Might the white dots be a migraine headache? Though he'd never had one before and his head wasn't aching.

He lay on the bed and tried to relax. He breathed as slowly as he could, trying to slow the rate of his heartbeat. Despite his anxiety and the churning question and formulations in his mind, his head turned into the pillow and he drifted some of the way towards sleep.

And on the threshold of sleep, he sees himself walking along a hospital corridor. As he passes each open doorway, the sudden warm smells of sickness. He is standing near a bank of elevators looking out of the window onto the flat, gravelled roof. The roof is mobbed with pigeons and seagulls screeching and squawking and fighting for the scraps thrown out of windows by patients and orderlies. The roof is seething with the bodies of birds. They tread upon each other. Pigeons are pecking cigarette butts and a dead pigeon. The gulls are threatening each other, pumping up raucous challenges. One rises to a piercing crescendo only for another to start over again. The screeching of the gulls heard through the glass merges with geriatric wailing further up the corridor, a cacophony of aggression, fear and despair.

He goes into the room. It has two beds in it but only one is occupied. The nurse is bent over the person in the bed. The sheets and blankets are pulled back off the bed and trail on the floor. The nurse plaps a sanitary napkin onto the polished linoleum. It is bloody. She withdraws a syringe and caps it and puts it on a stainless steel tray on the bedside table.

He goes around the bed and looks down at Sheila. Her eyes are closed. He puts his hand on her arm. It is cold and clammy. Karla is wearing a stethoscope. She looks up at him across the bed.

She shakes her head.

The room is silent. The only sound other than Sheila's rapid, shallow breathing is the screeching of birds.

THE BUS THAT HAD BEEN LAID ON FOR LJUBLJANA pulled out of the hotel car park onto the road that led to the highway. There were a dozen or so passengers from the conference, none that he'd spoken to before. He was returning to the Holiday Inn.

He'd woken only half an hour earlier and in a panic to catch the bus he'd forgone a shower, stuffed his possessions into his bag, paid the mini-bar bill at reception, and standing in the bar off the lobby, had gulped down a tepid black coffee.

The bus had been his only chance of getting into Ljubljana in time. He had agreed to give a lecture that afternoon at the

59

University of Ljubljana; yet another honorarium had been mentioned.

A few introductory ... the professor had said ... *and such and so.*

He gazed out of the window. His stomach was empty and rumbling and he still felt flustered from rushing about but at least he could *see*. The screen of white dots had disappeared entirely. He had Christopher's address in Sweden and he would write to him – and to Karla – to explain his disappearance the night before and his unceremonious departure.

The journey took just over an hour. The room that had been reserved for him was actually vacant and ready for occupation. He poured a package of Tide into the washbasin and washed the shirt he'd been too ill to deal with the night before. His flight the next day to Frankfurt left at eight in the morning. The trip to the airport took some twenty minutes to half an hour. He liked to be early so he would need a taxi at six-thirty. The hotel could doubtless supply one, but he had accepted a business card from the driver who had driven him in from the airport and had promised to phone him. He suspected the man was desperate for the business. The switchboard got him the number and eventually he made himself understood and completed the arrangements.

He went downstairs and ate breakfast in the Holiday Inn restaurant in solitary state. Four unenthusiastic waiters stood about. He worked his way through a mushroom omelette and three rolls with butter and plum jam and felt soothed and restored after the purging his stomach had suffered in the night. The morning fog was dispersing, the sun burning through. He decided that he would go for a walk along the Ljubljanica River and then devote the rest of the morning to finding presents for Sheila, Chris and Tony. As he strolled out into the plaza in front of the hotel, he was feeling a lightness of spirit, almost a jauntiness.

60

Presents for Chris and Tony would prove far more difficult than finding a present for Sheila. They seemed to be interested only in rock bands, basketball and strange fantasy magazines involving dragons, mazes, dungeons and monsters. Pleasant enough boys but he found them rather blank. Sheila said they'd turn out just fine, that all boys were like this. What he was seeing was just adolescent conformity. Beneath were two sturdy individuals. Forde trusted Sheila's understanding of people and did not doubt that she was right. What troubled him was what they didn't *know*. Things like History and Geography. Sheila had told him he was becoming cranky.

Two years previously he'd taken the pair of them to England to visit their grandparents. He had shown them Buckingham Palace, the Tower of London, the British Museum, Westminster Abbey, all the delights of London. He had taken them to Warwick Castle. To Stratford to see Shakespeare's birthplace. To Oxford. Through the Cotswold villages. Chris had been – he thought for a moment – eleven and Tony thirteen.

He had tried to give them a sense of the past, to connect them with it. He'd pointed out tumuli in the fields and medieval strips and baulks still visible under the turf. He had taken them through an iron-age hill fort. He'd marched them along the Ridgeway from the White Horse at Uffington to the megalithic long barrow called Wayland's Smithy, rhapsodizing the while that their feet were treading the same ground that tribes and armies had marched on since prehistory.

On their return to Canada, Chris had confided in Sheila that the place he'd liked most, the very best place they'd visited, was Fortnum and Mason. The high point of the expedition for Tony, apparently, had been the purchase of an extra-large T-shirt on the Charing Cross Road, a T-shirt bought without consultation, on which was printed front and back: Too Drunk To Fuck.

It was in the bookstore where he'd seen in the window the omnibus edition of Jalna novels by Mazo de la Roche that he happened upon the perfect gift for Sheila. The book was a facsimile edition in superb colour of a famous medieval Jewish book in the collection of the National Museum in Sarajevo. The book was in a slipcase which also contained a pamphlet in English detailing the book's history.

It was known now as the *Sarajevo Haggadah*. One hundred and forty-two vellum pages. The text was illuminated lavishly, initial words in gold and a blue so intense it might have been made with powdered lapis lazuli. Hebrew characters became flowers; heraldic and fanciful beasts stalked the intricate foliage. Just as beautiful was the chaste unadorned calligraphy of the prayers. The stories of the Exodus were illustrated with nearly a hundred miniature paintings.

The *Sarajevo Haggadah* was thought to have been written and painted most probably in Barcelona shortly after 1350. When the Jews were expelled from Spain in 1492, the book had started its journey eastward. There was a record of it in Italy in 1609. It was carried into the Balkans, most probably to Split or Dubrovnik by a family called Kohen. The book was sold to the National Museum in Sarajevo in 1894.

He was touched that reproduced on some pages were the spots and blotches from wine and food spilled on the book during Seders over the centuries. And it pleased him to think that next Passover when they went to Toronto for the Seder, Sheila would be able to read along in something more sumptuous than the prayer books her father handed out and her father would be able to pontificate on the historical prohibition against art in sacred texts in the Jewish tradition and when he discovered the book was Sephardic he would launch into rambling assaults on Ladino as a language and the eccentricity, if not impurity, of Sephardic rites and Sheila's mother would either contradict him or introduce a new topic of conversation she'd derived from TV talk shows such as the spontaneous combustion of human beings and within minutes everyone would be shouting and on it would go, on and on it would go....

AT SIX-THIRTY HE WAS WAITING IN THE LOBBY with his carry-on bag, his briefcase and his furled umbrella. The night had passed restfully and without incident. He had not bothered with breakfast as it would be served on the plane and he'd be able to get coffee at the airport.

He was brooding about his carry-on bag. Because he was up early, the collar and cuffs of his shirt were still slightly damp and clammy. He had worn the same shirt every day except for the day before when migraine or whatever it had been had prevented his washing it. But it was obvious that, normal circumstances prevailing, one shirt would suffice. If he were to cut out seconds on socks and underpants as well, it might be possible to get essentials into a briefcase alone. He stood looking out of the plate glass window. It was slightly foggy again. Not enough to delay take-off, he hoped. Checked his watch. He thought it would be something of a triumph if he could dispense with a carry-on bag, if he could get into his briefcase alone any necessary papers and the essentials – toothbrush, toothpaste, hairbrush, *Hart's Rules*, razor, cellophane twists of Tide, aspirins. Light glowed on the fog. The taxi turned into the plaza and drew up under the porte-cochère.

The driver greeted him warmly and they shook hands. As they cleared Ljubljana itself, the fog seemed to be thinning. They'd been driving along for about fifteen minutes when the car slowed and the driver signalled a left turn. Forde listened to the click-click-click of the indicator. The driver turned off the main road and into a narrow side road.

63

'Is this the way to the airport?' said Forde.

The driver raised his forefinger and nodded, a gesture obviously meaning: Just be patient. Wait for a minute. At the bottom of the hill, the driver pulled up onto the grass verge. Forde felt slightly apprehensive. He hoped he wasn't being set up. He looked at his watch. They got out and Forde followed the driver along the road until they came to a stone bridge. The driver put his finger to his lips and then gestured for Forde to stoop. They approached the centre of the bridge bent almost double and then rose slowly to peer over the side.

The river was quite wide and mist hung over it. In the middle of the river was a long narrow island. Standing at the near end of the island were two cranes and some little distance behind them a nest, a great platform of gathered sedge and reeds.

The cranes were bowing to each other, their heads coming down close to the ground. One of the birds fanned out its bustle of tail plumes and started to strut circles around the other, every now and then leaning in towards it sideways as if to gather or impart intimacies. Then the crane with the raised plumes walked over to the messy nest and began to parade around it, pausing from time to time to bow deeply towards it.

The other bird raised its great wings over its back and jumped into the air. The other responded by launching itself sideways, a collapsing, hopping jump. The jumps looked like the hopeless efforts of a flightless bird to take wing. They started jumping together. There was something comic in the spectacle. It was as if these huge and stately birds were being deliberately juvenile and ungainly. The way they trailed their legs suggested the way dancers in musicals jump and click their heels together in the air. Their antics were oddly incongruous. The birds were so regal, so dignified that to see them flap and hop and topple was as if two portly prelates in gaiters suddenly started to caper and prance.

One of them stretched its long heron-like neck straight up into the air and gave forth a great trumpet blast of noise, harsh and unbelievably loud.

Krraaa-krro.

The other bird straightened the S of its neck and replied.

Krraaa-krro.

And then the two birds paced towards each other until their breasts were touching and began to rub each other's necks with their heads, long swooping and rising caresses, their beaks nuzzling at the height of the embrace.

The driver took out a packet of cigarettes and lit one. Forde realized that his fingers were clenched over the edge of the stone block. The smell of tobacco hung on the air.

The driver grinned at Forde.

Forde smiled back.

The cranes trumpeted at the sky, first one then the fierce reply, reverberating blasts of noise bouncing off the stonework of the bridge filling the air with the clamour of jubilation.

Forde felt …

Forde exulted with them.

John Metcalf was born in Carlisle, England, and was educated at the University of Bristol. He emigrated to Canada in 1962. In addition to working on his own writings (novels, stories and essays), he holds the unsalaried post of Senior Editor of the Porcupine's Quill, and is the editor of *Canadian Notes & Queries*. *Forde Abroad* was originally published in story form by *The New Quarterly* and won the National Magazine Awards Gold Medal for Fiction in 1996. Metcalf's memoir, *An Aesthetic Underground*, was published by Patrick Crean at Thomas Allen in the spring of 2003.

Novellas Uniform With This Volume

The Deep by Mary Swan (2002)

The Stand-In by David Helwig (2002)